ZOE
RISING

ZOE RISING

Pam Conrad

A TRUMPET CLUB SPECIAL EDITION

ISBN 0-590-36319-0

12 11 10 9 8 7 6 5 4 3 2   3 4 5 6 7 8 9/0

Printed in the U.S.A.   40
First Scholastic printing, October 1997

ZOE
RISING

PROLOGUE

Whenever I wake in the morning to hear summer crows, I always think I am in the bedroom of my grandmother's house. I will probably always think I am Zoe, a small girl waking up in that room. I'm aware, even as it is happening, that there can be no truth to it, that the sensation is just an illusion of time, but knowing this never changes things.

Even if I make myself open my eyes and look around in other rooms, other times, I know one thing: The most memorable mornings are crafted of the same stuff—trees carved like Victorian silhouettes against pale glowing skies; wet grasses calling to be walked on by small wispy ghosts; and crows—always crows, calling to one another in the early hours. They are like stagehands wandering across an empty stage, frequently startled by the apparition of actor-ghosts rising up from the mist. I know because I had seen how they had been startled by me tiptoeing, wet footed and spooky, across their grassy mornings.

It was during those early years, those early mornings, that I'd become accustomed to the habits of crows and the ways of ghosts, so that when the time came once more, I did not hesitate to slip out of my body. I would know once again the simple sudden terror of the crows that lifted us fierce and rigid into the treetops and sent us scrambling along a horizon of leafy twigs and weak branches.

In the summer of my fourteenth year I left my body willingly, feet first, rose high into the sky above lake and bay, and went somewhere I was not supposed to go.

No. It was not somewhere. It was sometime. And I need to tell it now.

ONE

It happened in the long, final summer days at Camp Cedar Ravine where I had gone with my best friend, a mainland boy named Jedidiah. After being there so long, I had lost all track of time, feeling as though I would just live on there forever. Then early one morning, a group of us older campers marched down to the lake as we had many times before. There, with packaged breakfasts, we would all paddle sleepily to the other side of the lake, and then eat and explore the beach. On each expedition there, I had found neat things, things to line up on my windowsill back at the cabin—old shells, an abandoned nest, and even a starfish, which Monty said was impossible at the lake. It was a five-pointed starfish, rough to the touch, with a small V-shaped gouge in one of its stout triangular legs. A starfish was a sea creature, not a lake creature, he said. Someone must have brought it from a beach and left it there. But this didn't matter to me. If anything, it endeared it to me all the more, because like me, the starfish was in an unexpected place. I brought it back to my cabin with me anyway, a summer keepsake.

Monty was our counselor, a college boy who'd been coming to Camp Cedar Ravine since he was a little boy. They'd even named one of the hills we climbed "Monty's Mountain" out of affection for him. He was a champion swimmer, an excellent canoer, and I was interested to see how he blushed around the girl counselors.

Monty liked to sing, and everywhere we went we had to listen to him. He didn't sing old camp songs that we knew and could join in on; no, he'd make up things as he went along. Mostly they were stupid things that made us laugh, but other times we'd get quiet and listen, despite ourselves.

This one particular morning he'd been singing something about his feet taking him down to the river, something crazy about his toes making holes in his patent-leather boots. Jedidiah and I walked side by side: Jed used to Monty, barely listening, and me trying to remember every word to put in my letters home to Grandma.

I had never been to camp before, and never would have had a chance to go at all if it hadn't been for Jedidiah, who'd gone just about every summer for his whole life. In our fourteenth summer Jedidiah refused to go. He told his parents he was too old. Said he'd had enough campfires and canoe trips and mosquitoes, and he wouldn't go. He wanted to stay home and maybe get a job, or row across the bay to visit me. His parents told him he must go. There would be no arguing. It was non-negotiable, but they knew their son well, and they offered him a tempting bribe that—to my absolute delight—Jedidiah accepted.

They told him that if he would like, and if my grandparents approved, they would assume the expense of sending me along with Jedidiah to

Camp Cedar Ravine in southern Maine. When he first told me, we whooped with joy. He would be the veteran camper, showing me the ropes and introducing me to the wilds of Maine. And I would be the novice, the empty notebook waiting to be filled. I know it was an odd time in our lives for a boy and girl to be such good friends, but in truth there was nothing romantic about our attachment to each other. We had been close for years.

The other kids at the camp seemed to understand this, and all summer long they accepted me as Jedidiah's special friend, almost as his sister or cousin, I suppose. We did just about everything side by side, and I was comfortable that way. I was slow to make friends and wasn't so sure I wanted to be paired off for events with some girl I didn't know or trust. But the girls didn't hesitate to flirt with Jedidiah in front of me and then confide in me that they thought he was the cutest. I would listen stone-faced and then tease him later.

We all dragged our canoes down to the water that morning, and Jedidiah and I were the first out on the lake. Because we were strong, and used to rowing PopPop's skiff together, we had pulled ahead of the others and were almost near the opposite shore. I grinned at the back of his head, at his lopping wheat-colored curls that the girls loved.

"Danielle thinks you're to die for," I told him. It took ten full strokes for his ears to reach their peak redness. "How about you? You like her?"

"Which one is she again?" he asked, and I laughed.

"You are terrible!" I said, putting more weight into my paddle. I glanced out at the others. We were way ahead of everyone. Too far ahead. Oddly, it seemed they were turning around and heading back. "Where's everyone going?" I asked.

"I was just going to ask you the same thing," he said, and we stopped paddling and coasted, peering at the distant shore, watching the other canoes circling round. Someone was standing at the shore. Three blasts on a whistle.

"Three blasts. Emergency return." Jedidiah turned and looked at me. "I wonder what's up?"

I looked at the sky and around at the horizon. "I

don't see a storm coming. No thunderheads, no funnel clouds."

"Must be something else," he mused. "Damn. We just got out here. What a pain."

Jedidiah began to paddle steadily, and I held my paddle deep in the water and we turned on its axis. "So, you didn't answer, Jedi-die-for. What do you think of Danielle?"

"I think girls are too weird," he said. "Too intense. I hate how they look in your eyes like they're trying to make you say something against your will."

"*I* don't do that," I said. I smiled and stared into the glare of the water. I smiled, but I remembered how Zoe Louise, the ghost I had once known, used to stare into my eyes for long stretches of time. "I *never* do that," I declared. "Ever." Anymore.

"I didn't say you did."

We could see everyone hopping out of their canoes, pulling them up on the shore. Monty was walking away with one of the boys. I remember thinking at the time that it was Carney, Carney the one who had been so boisterous at dinner last night. He and Monty were talking intently.

"You're not a regular girl," Jedidiah was telling me as we pulled the canoe up on the pebbly beach. The rest of the campers were gathering around Amanda, whose face, I saw as we got closer, was pinched and worried.

"Sit down here a minute," she was saying. She turned and glanced into the woods to the path that Monty and Carney had taken. At that instant the woods seemed to burst into a gut-wrenching cry that made everyone jump. I expected Amanda to go after them, but when I looked at her, there was something else in her eyes. She knew the reason for the scream. "Come sit in a circle," she ordered, and hugging her arms around herself, she lowered her head as if bracing for a dive. I remained standing behind everyone.

"What's going on?" Jedidiah asked.

"Something terrible has happened," Amanda said. "Last night. We just found out about it. Carney's uncle just arrived. Carney's parents were both killed last night in a car accident."

There was a gasp and then total stillness, whispers. "Oh, no." "Oh, my God." "Oh, Carney." Some

9

of the campers began to cry. Two of the girls held each other, and one of the boys got up and began walking in the direction in which Carney had disappeared.

"Sit down, Ben."

"I've got to go to him. He's my best friend."

"Later, Ben. Let the counselors talk to him first. Then, you'll be able to see him before he leaves."

Ben sat abruptly on the beach, his hands in fists, frowning.

One of the girls began sobbing. "I want to call my mother. I want to make sure she's okay!"

Grandma. . . . PopPop. . . . I suddenly thought of them with a shudder.

Amanda went to her and hugged her. "That's understandable, sweetie. But your Mom's fine, believe me. You don't have to worry about her."

"Grandma. . . . PopPop. . . ." I whispered.

Later they would all remember it as the first time I fainted. That's what they called it—a fainting spell. But it was not that. I had been seized with a deep ache for Carney, his parents suddenly gone without ever saying a forever good-bye. I had thought how he'd never see their faces or hear their voices again, and then I thought of my grandparents, and it happened.

Before that moment, whenever I'd thought of being so far away from Grandma and PopPop, I had quivered with excitement, or a kind of nervousness. I wouldn't have called it fear before. It had been like sparkling Jell-O at first, sweet, warm, and liquid, but now it hardened into a quaking cube, and later still, it would become a granite block of terror. I was suddenly overwhelmed with alarm about Grandma and PopPop. I felt as though without me there to be a part of their day, to anchor them in that house, they would disintegrate and die. I never should have left them. They would die without me.

I was standing on the pebbled shore with everyone all around me, and yet oddly, without closing my eyes, I could see my grandmother right in front of me. I was standing before her, and yet I was invisible to her. She was wearing her black-and-white-checked apron and folding laundry on the back porch, pulling things out of the basket where she had tossed them from the line and she was folding them. I knew this was exactly what she was doing that instant. She was safe. She was okay.

I looked around desperately for PopPop and saw him getting out of his truck in the driveway. I felt myself run to him, call to him, "PopPop!" but my voice seemed far away, and when I reached out to slip my hand into his, my hand passed through him, feeling the coolness as his ring slipped through the bones of my hand. "PopPop! PopPop!" I called, but he didn't hear me. I watched as he lifted an old beaten suitcase into the back of the truck and swatted at a yellow jacket that darted around his head. Then he faded away.

I stood on grass, on pebbles, stunned. What had happened to me once before was happening again. I could hear the crows caw overhead. Panic rose in my throat as if my canoe had suddenly swamped.

"PopPop," I whispered, barely able to breathe. "PopPop." I kept saying that over and over until I saw that Amanda was shaking me, calling to me. And then I realized I wasn't standing in the grass looking at my grandparents. I was looking up into the trees. Into the sky. I was lying on the ground. I was flat on my back on pebbles.

TWO

You might think I am strange. You would not be the first to think that. But you are the first I have tried to explain myself to, the first I have tried to convince that I am not so strange at all.

I had lived with Grandma and PopPop since I was four years old, and they had never seemed worried about me growing up on the island, where there were no other children. And for my part, I don't ever remember feeling this was odd, or that their house was a lonely place. No, it was a safe haven, full of the ways they knew to love me. They allowed me an absolute, tangible freedom that most children never know: They never once asked what I was thinking.

I could sit in the tree out back all day long, watching the shade stretch first to the west and then to the east, and they would never question what I was doing. My grandmother would just bring me apples and crackers and say it was amazing how I could go so long without a bathroom. My occasional fits of brooding silence were welcomed moments of peace and quiet to them. And the ghost that haunted my early years was—to my old grandparents—a friend of my lonely imagination, and they thought they humored me by calling her Zoe Louise.

My first experiences of friendship with real living children were limited to the school I attended on the mainland during the fall and winter months. PopPop thought nothing of rowing me over in the skiff each morning and back again each afternoon to save the cost of the ferry. He would do this to make sure I attended school—and although I never heard him complain all the years I was with him, it never once occurred to him to row me over to visit a friend.

My classmates would be released at the sound of the bell after a long day, and they would spill out of the building into the schoolyard. There I would see all the young mothers waiting together like geese at the gate. I would watch jealously the way they scolded their children, zippered their open jackets, and tucked in scarves around their necks and mittens into sleeves. And then I would watch as they said good-bye to one another and headed off to what I imagined to be their perfect houses, where my classmates would eat pretzels and chocolate and sing songs with their fathers. PopPop would smile, take my hand and lead me to the dock.

I was the outsider, the outcast, and I never understood the ways of other children, especially when suddenly my outcast rank miraculously changed to a position of celebrity. Jedidiah must have told the other children what he saw, and somehow they must have decided I was a child of infinite freedoms; and although I never let on to them, perhaps they could even sense I was a treader of other times.

I know exactly the day it happened. I was in the fourth grade. I had gone to that same school ever since first grade and no one had ever asked where I went at the end of each day. No one had noticed that I was not in their neighborhood, and that they didn't see me in their churches or at their violin classes.

It was a foggy afternoon late in autumn and PopPop and I were returning to the island a little later than usual because we had stopped for groceries. I was waiting on the dock next to the boat while he arranged the parcels across the stern when I heard my name.

"Zoe?"

It was Jedidiah, and I knew him then only as the boy who sat in the seat in front of me that year. I lifted my hand to him and smiled timidly.

His mother stood behind him in a long woolen coat. "Come along, Jed," she said.

"Where are you going, Zoe?" he asked, ignoring her, standing surefooted and stubborn on the dock.

"Home," I told him.

"Where do you live?"

I pointed into the fog.

"The island? You live on the island and you come to school each day in that boat?"

PopPop was suddenly quiet, and I knew he was listening. I nodded, awkward and uncertain in my embarrassment, but I didn't take my eyes off Jedidiah, and I watched in pleased amazement as his whole countenance swelled with admiration. "I would like that. You're so lucky," he said.

I smiled and looked at PopPop, who smiled back at me.

"I would like to visit you," Jedidiah stated.

Visit me! It had never occurred to me before that someone would like to visit me.

"Maybe someday you can come for dinner," PopPop was saying, nodding at Jed's mother, who stepped forward and tapped Jed's shoulder impatiently.

"Maybe," she said, not unkindly. "Come on now, Jed. Daddy's waiting." She turned and walked off, secure, I guess, in her knowledge that Jed would follow after her, but Jed stayed on the dock watching us.

17

PopPop held out his hand to me. I boarded the boat and took my usual position at the bow. Then PopPop drew in the lines and shoved us away from the dock. I waved steadily, back and forth without stopping, like a pendulum on a clock, as my grandfather began to row me backward into the fog.

I could see Jedidiah watching me intently. I knew he was seeing me with new eyes. I have never asked him what he thought of me then, but from that day on, I stopped thinking of myself as the poor little girl who lived on the island. I was suddenly the lucky girl who sailed away each day on a skiff.

I waved back and forth, my face a-twitch with my effort not to smile, and I knew I looked excellent disappearing into the fog.

This was the beginning of my unusual friendship with Jedidiah. He was as exotic to me with his two parents, three older brothers, and a station wagon as I was to him with my solitary island home and my daily cruise across the lower bay with my old grandfather.

Once or twice a month during the school year I was invited to have dinner at Jedidiah's house, to observe up close what brothers were like, a father, and a mother who laughed and sat down with us, who drove us to the movies, and set a table. I was like a scientist studying a rare species from close range. Jedidiah always insisted on going with me when it was time for his father to drive me to the dock, and there they would stay on the dock and watch PopPop and me skim out into the darkness, silently, in the nightshine, heading to the island.

Less frequently Jedidiah was allowed to come to the island, although his mother preferred he take the ferry, so it was usually on Saturdays that he was able to come, and I would meet him at the ferry port on my bike; and then, in various combinations of the two of us sitting on the seat, the crossbar, the handlebars, pedaling or not, laughing wildly, we would make our way to my grandparents' house.

Jedidiah, with his high energy and enthusiasm for my life, became my best friend, and while he was not my only friend, he was the first, and he was the only one who ever came regularly to the island, the only one who called my grandparents— for all their lives—Grandma and PopPop.

And Jedidiah was the only one in those days that I ever spoke to about what had happened with my mother. He knew how she'd left me at my grandparents' house when I was four years old, so long ago it was not worth remembering, yet I could not forget. I had told Jedidiah how her hands were always cold, and how she hugged Grandma's dog in a way she'd never hugged me. And how she used to come to the island once or twice a year, not to see me, or at least it never felt like that, but it seemed she came to be in the house for a little while, to sit in the familiar chairs, stand before the remembered sink, and stroke the dog. Then leave.

I worried that someday Jedidiah might be there when she arrived, and I tried to prepare him for her odd appearance—the layers of scarves, the wilted hats, and the dark and mysterious capes— but he was more interested in whether or not I resembled her. I admitted that, yes, anyone could tell by looking at our faces that she was my mother, but no, I was nothing like her. And then perhaps to prove this to him as well as myself I would become very conscious of the way I spoke and acted—moving quickly and confidently, making myself aware of Jedidiah's presence and the substance of our time with each other as she never was with me.

Jedidiah was the only one I ever told of my secret wish, that she would somehow change, that she'd show up one day transformed and willing to take on the task of being a *true mother* to me.

Without knowing what was in store, and believing as he did that all parents had to be basically good and loving, Jedidiah tried to reassure me by telling me that one day my mother would probably surprise me.

But I never believed in good surprises then. I was sure that at any moment something terrible would finally happen. I remember watering my grandmother's houseplants, and on dry days I'd watch the water's surface tension bulge above the soil of the plant, holding, holding, and then, with one sliver of water, break over the edge of the clay pot, bringing all the water after it. I used to think life was that delicate, that easy to break.

That is probably why when Carney's parents died, I didn't trust that his loss would not spill over the edge and take my grandparents with it.

THREE

The camp buildings at Cedar Ravine were unusually quiet that night. The branches of the trees were still, pressed flat against the sunset, no wind, no birds. It was the kind of still PopPop would have watched guardedly, to see what it would turn into. A storm perhaps. The cabins were empty. We all knew that Carney's bunk was cleaned out and his shelves were bare. Ben hadn't come to dinner and Danielle whispered at the table that he wanted to go home, he didn't want to stay. I wanted to go home too, and wondered if Ben's parents would come for him. Maybe I could go with him. He could take me home.

I was moving the rice pudding around in its bowl, staring into space, when Monty came over to where we, the older campers, were sitting and tapped his spoon lightly on the table. He had an announcement. "I know this is against our usual deal here, but we had an idea that maybe you'd all sleep a little better tonight if you could call home and talk to your parents."

There was a murmur of yeses.

"All right, we have to do this in some kind of order. It's a nice enough night, so why don't we build a campfire and then we'll call you in one or two at a time to use the phone and call home."

Amanda came up beside him, nodding, and looking at each of our faces.

"Jed. Zoe," she said. "You be in charge of collecting firewood and Lance, here's a list of everyone. You be in charge of checking off when each person has called home—"

I followed Jedidiah out of the mess hall into the back field, feeling restless and impatient. I realized Jed was looking at me funny.

"What?" I asked.

"Are you all right now?" he asked.

"I'm fine. I was fine all along."

"You fainted," he reminded me. "You looked weird."

I knew I hadn't fainted. I looked at him, and it crossed my mind to tell him what had really happened to me, what I had seen. And then to go on and tell him how this was not new to me, how once before I had left my body and gone to another time, where I had eaten raspberries and chased a ghost who had stolen my doll. No. I couldn't tell him that. I didn't think then I'd ever be able to tell him that.

"I got scared," I told him truthfully. "I thought of my grandparents. And how they're all I have."

He stopped and turned to me. "My parents are all *I* have and *I* didn't pass out."

"They are *not* all you have," I told him. "They're your real parents, not something you got when you lost your parents, and you've got brothers and—"

"All right!"

"You don't know what it's like to just have grandparents who are old anyway to start out, and

25

you worry all the time that they might fall or get sick."

"Simmer down, Zoe. I hear you. I get it."

I was so angry at him. "I don't think you do!"

"Why are you so defensive about fainting?"

"'Cause I didn't faint!"

"You did too."

I could have punched him. Leveled him right there in the grass. I was so alone with this, this thing that had happened to me again. "I didn't faint," I told him. "I went home."

He looked at me funny. His mouth twitched. He reached out and tapped on my head. "Knock. Knock. You in there?"

I pushed his hand away. "You can ask my grandparents yourself. I saw them. Grandma was folding laundry on the porch, and PopPop was getting out of the truck."

"Sounds like a normal day to me!"

"She was wearing her black-and-white apron."

He grinned. "And my mother was wearing her yellow sweatshirt."

"I'll bet she wasn't."

"And my father was polishing the car."

"Bet he wasn't." I stuck out my pinkie. "I'll bet you my grandfather was getting out of the truck, and a yellow jacket was bothering him. Bet?"

Jedidiah rolled his eyes.

"And I'll bet your mother was not wearing her yellow sweatshirt and your father didn't polish the car today." I kept jabbing him with my pinkie until finally he locked his pinkie in it and shook.

"All right! All right! It's a bet." We walked off toward the wood stack on the side of the building. We butted shoulders, testing our strength against each other. "How much?" he asked.

"How much what?"

"How much do we bet?"

"Bag of chips," I said, already regretting I had told him.

"Bag of chips," he agreed.

It grew very dark that night. There were no stars, only a slice of a moon that appeared intermittently from behind stormy black clouds. And a breeze was building, buffeting us now and then with cold gusts. We all huddled together around the swirling, sputtering fire and took turns going alphabetically to the counselor cabin where the phone was. One or two campers at a time would drift off, bouncing a flashlight beam ahead of them. The rest of us spooked ourselves. I was surprised that Monty and Amanda didn't stop it when it started, that they let it go so far, but it seemed inevitable.

We began a ghost story, the kind where one person starts and stops, and the next person has to pick it up and continue. Our faces were like jack-o'-lanterns, our noses shadowed against our foreheads, our cheeks sending blurs of darkness over our eyes. "It was a dark and stormy night," someone began, "and the naked bloody bodies began slithering through the woods, *ka-clump, ka-clump, ka-clump,* coming to kill the children, the little children, the big children, whoever they could find, to tear out and eat their hearts and throw their brains—"

Next.

"And throw their brains into the lake. Then in

the fog their ghosts would rise and come back again to claim more children. And the ghost children went looking for their parents. They waited till their parents were on elevators, then they cut the cables. They waited till their parents were on ships and then they sank them. They huddled on the sides of roads and jumped out and made the cars swerve and crash over cliffs. And then the parents—"

Next.

"Then the parents, two by two, came out of the woods, hungry for blood and brains and revenge. They would kill all the children who were ever angry at their parents. They would chop up anyone who had ever talked back. They would burn children who smoked cigarettes, and drown ones who drank whiskey, and torture—"

Next.

"Ninety-nine Cherokee Jeeps on the road, ninety-nine Cherokee Jeeps." It was Monty. "If one of the Jeeps should go to the mall, ninety-eight Cherokee Jeeps on the road. Ninety-eight Cherokee Jeeps on the road—" We all joined in, no one smiling. No one taking their eyes off the shadows walking against the cabins, the bouncing beams of flashlights traveling back and forth.

When it was Jedidiah's turn I went with him. We sat together on the desk while he dialed and then I listened as he talked to his mother.

"Yeah, they let us call because we found out one of the campers's parents died last night. . . . Everybody's upset. . . . They let us call. . . . Carney, it was Carney's parents. Yeah, from New Jersey. . . . Yeah. . . ."

I nudged him. Stared in his eyes. *Ask her,* I mouthed silently.

He nodded and closed his eyes to shut me out. "No, I'm okay. . . . You're okay, right?" Jedidiah laughed a little. "I knew you were okay. Some of the kids were upset." He opened his eyes and looked at me. "Zoe fainted." I stood up and glared at him.

"Would you ask her!" I hissed.

"All right. All right. Mom?" He held out his hand to me. "I have a bet with Zoe. Tell me the truth. Were you wearing your yellow sweatshirt today?" He frowned.

"And your father," I whispered.

"No? Well, how about Dad? Did he wash the car today?" His eyebrows met in a scowl. "Nah. Nothing. Just a bet Zoe and I had. Yeah. Dumb bet. Now I owe her a bag of chips."

I slapped the air in triumph, anxious to call Grandma and prove that she'd worn her black-and-white apron, and that PopPop had been bothered by a yellow jacket by the truck, but when Jedidiah finally hung up and we dialed my grandparents' number, no one answered.

It didn't make sense. My grandparents never went anywhere. They did the same thing every night for years and years—sat in their chairs in the living room, PopPop smoking his pipe, Grandma crocheting, every night for years. No one answered the phone. It rang and rang and rang. I dialed their number five times while I was with Jedidiah and then a few more times before everyone went off to their bunks. Monty told me I could try again in the morning.

As the wind picked up outside, and the trees scratched against the sides of our cabin, I thought nervously of the old beaten suitcase I was so sure I had seen PopPop loading into the truck. I was filled with dread. Were they all right?

I lay awake in the darkness of the cabin listening to the murmur of the other girls breathing in their sleep. In those other days, when I had first ghost-walked, I had always passed through time and space by going up the back staircase at my grandparents' home. I would not have thought there was any other way, and I would not have even thought about going to my grandparents' on pure will alone, except that I had had the experience on the pebbled beach that morning, where I left my body without the staircase, without anything. Perhaps it was because I was older now. Perhaps ghost-walking was a thing that I could perfect and master, like swimming or writing reports.

I tried thinking of cicadas, and I willed myself to slough off my body the way they did, leaving it dry and empty on my bunk. I grew tense from the effort. I couldn't do it. How had I done it earlier, out under the trees on the pebbled beach, in the bright morning daylight?

I kept trying to recapture what had happened. As though squinting into a mist, I tried to see my grandmother's face. I tried to block out the sounds of the girls, the branches on the roof of the cabin, and I listened for PopPop's voice. Nothing.

Then, when it seemed nothing would work, and I let go of all effort, waves of terror overtook me. I *had* to see my grandparents. I *had* to know they were all right. And I suppose it was the fear that finally did it.

It felt as though stiff salty lines were wound around my soul's ankles, and I was brutally yanked, lifted up by my feet, upside down, awkward, dangerous. And then, before I could turn timid and change my mind, I willed myself home.

FOUR

*E*arlier, in the first days of my ghost-walking, slipping out of my skin had usually led me to daylight hours, brightness, sweetness, a safe place. So I had not anticipated being plunged into darkness, and I wandered aimlessly and frightened for a while, before I recognized the place I had stumbled upon. Ahead of me were the trees that grew behind Grandma's barn, and on the other side of the barn were the lights coming from the rear of the house. Even though I walked forward quickly, the ground was dragging beneath me, slower than my feet were moving, making me feel that I was too heavy, too cumbersome to move through such darkness.

At first I had been relieved by the sight of the house with its shining lights and promised warmth. My grandparents were home after all. But even as I felt that relief I felt an odd twinge of uneasiness. Something wasn't right. My bare feet were an autumn breeze, kicking up the leaves in swirling circles. Autumn leaves, dry, deep red and yellow, swirling about my bare feet, my tan bare summer feet. Autumn leaves crunching. It was all wrong.

"Grandma?" I called out. I was trying to run. The ground did not feel firm beneath my feet, but shifty, as though the grass could suddenly be withdrawn, sending me hurtling away. The living-room light was bright, and I ran right up to the window and looked in through the fine lace curtains. PopPop was in his chair, and across from him Grandma was sitting with some orange fabric in her lap. They were laughing. PopPop was waving his hands in the air.

I was about to knock on the windowpane when I saw a little girl run into the room, drawn by their laughter, and stand by my grandfather's chair, smiling up into his face, attentive to his story. He kept on talking to my grandmother, seeming to ignore the child; but then, without taking his eyes off my grandmother's face, he scooped the child up and put her in his lap. I was startled to see her wind her small arms around his neck. Who was this?

I rapped on the window. "PopPop! It's me."

He went on talking and now I could hear my grandmother's laughter as well.

I knocked hard. Harder.

They didn't hear me. But the little girl suddenly turned toward me, attentive and alert. I thought how if she'd been a small animal she would have perched up on her hind legs and turned small erect ears in my direction. Then without a word, she slid off PopPop's lap and came to the window. I saw her small hand grip the curtain and lift it aside as she ducked under it. She cupped her hands around her eyes and peered out into my darkness.

Now I have already told you about my mother— how there was an emptiness in her eyes. She was like those Easter eggs Grandma and I used to paint. Before painting them we would prick little pin-holes in each end and blow out the liquid egg. My mother was like that—a blown-out egg, the form hard and there, but in truth, hollow and fragile. I had never known my mother to be any other way. And yet I knew there must have been a time when she was not like that, when she was still full and whole.

And now, I stared as the little girl peered out into the yard, the edges of her hands white and flat against the windowpane. Stunned, I couldn't take my eyes off her. She was so full and whole.

And then my mother waved at me.

Later it seemed that as I stumbled backward, that I tripped, or somehow lost my grip on the moment that held me at the window. I was suddenly cupped in the bowl of a large ladle, whipped around viciously, then flung. As I was hurling through yesterdays and befores, I felt the branches that scratched the roof of the cabin scrape along my face. Rain was pounding on the roof and beneath its pounding I heard the soft sleeping breaths of my cabin mates churn, then gasp. I lay crumbled against the inside wall of the cabin, beneath the window. In the darkness I could see their eyes peering at me. Small light beams clicked on, trembled along the floor.

"What is it?" one asked sleepily.

"What happened?" asked another, slipping from her bed and coming to me.

"Has she fainted again?"

"No. It's nothing. Nothing at all," I tried to say. But my cheeks were bleeding, and as I tried to stand, the world went black.

It was Amanda who was at my side when I gained consciousness. I was lying flat in my bunk beneath my blanket and she was pressing a packet of ice against my cheek. She held it away from my face when I opened my eyes and looked at her. Her face was dark with something I didn't understand.

"What happened?" I asked.

"I was just going to ask you the same thing, sweetie. Why were you out wandering around in the middle of the night without your flashlight?"

"Wandering around? No." How could I explain? "I—I—was right here."

She frowned. "Did you have to go to the bathroom? Is that it?"

I looked around at the girls in their bunks, peeking out at me from under their blankets.

"I didn't hear the door open," one of them said.

"Me neither," said another.

But Amanda reached out and pulled a brittle leaf out of my rain-drenched hair. "Do you sleepwalk, Zoe? Do you think that might be it?"

I shrugged. "I don't think so."

She pressed the ice pack back against my cheek and it stung. "You've got a pretty good scrape on your cheek," she told me. "And a bruise too, it looks like. Try to sleep now."

I pulled my blanket up around my chin. Home. I thought of the window in the darkness and my mother's face pressed to the glass, looking for me. How could I tell Amanda any of this? Had she ever wondered what her mother was like as a young child? Wished she could really see her as she was then? And not just in a photograph but right in front of her, breathing and looking back at her? Amanda would not have understood. No one

39

would have understood that once that thought took hold of me, it began to torture me like a late-night summer mosquito who wants only my ear, the deep inner dark of my ear.

Amanda was studying me. And then she said gently, "As soon as it's light, Zoe, you can call home."

In the morning, as soon as the sun cracked through the hills, I went to the counselors' cabin, where they poured me a glass of juice and let me dial my grandparents' number over and over again. I listened to it ring, imagined the phone ringing on the wall in the kitchen, square and black with its long knotted cord that PopPop would untangle once in a while.

"Do you have any idea where they might have gone?" Monty asked.

I shook my head. "They never go anywhere."

"They're okay, you know. I'm sure they're okay."

I glared at him.

"Zoe!" he said. "What are the chances of something happening to two families? It's impossible. Just the odds are impossible."

Amanda came in the door at that moment carrying some cartons. "No luck?" she asked.

I shook my head, and Monty began picking up books and straightening things as though he were suddenly impatient with me. "There must be a reason," he was saying. I was dialing the number again.

"But she's worried," Amanda said quietly.

Same thing. The endless ringing.

"Can I go home?" I asked. "Is Ben going home? Can I go with him?"

"Ben's not going home," Amanda said, looking at Monty. I knew she was telling him too. "He decided to stay."

"Then can I call Jedidiah's parents and ask them to check on my grandparents, find out where they are?"

Monty tossed the pile on the table. "Now, that's a good idea. Why didn't I think of that?"

"Can I now?" I held out the phone and at Amanda's nod, I dialed Jedidiah's house. Then, unlike the ringing that had gone on and on at my house, his mother answered at the first ring.

"Hello."

"Mrs. Seger?"

"Zoe? Is that you? What's wrong?"

"I can't seem to reach my grandparents," I told her. "I dial and dial and nobody's home. I can't believe nobody's home. They never go away. Who'd watch Oscar? Where would they go?"

"Oh, I'm sure there's a good answer," she said, her voice gentle and comforting, but I was not comforted.

"Where would they go?"

"Would you like me to go over there and check, honey? I could catch the next ferry. I'll go down there right now."

"Yes. And you'll call me back?"

"Right away," she promised.

FIVE

*A*fter leaving the counselors' building, I began to walk to the mess hall in a dark mood. Danielle fell in silently beside me. She followed along even though I avoided the worn path and walked through the grasses that brushed my legs and were just deep enough to reach my fingers.

"How's your face?" she finally asked, turning to look at me.

I answered by tilting my head and showing her the scrape.

"I used to sleepwalk," she told me. "It goes away sooner or later. I'd wake up suddenly and I'd be standing in the middle of the living room with my parents laughing at me. They had to tie a bell on my door so they'd wake up if I started walking in the middle of the night."

"Yeah, well then I guess you'd all better tie a bell around my neck so that you can keep track of me."

Suddenly Danielle gasped and threw herself on the grassy ground. She reached up and pulled me down beside her. "Shh! Shh!" she hissed. There, close to the ground, we were invisible, blending into the grasses to anyone looking across the field. It was cool and bright, quiet. Nearby a bird fluttered up and flew off.

"What?" I asked. "What is it?"

"Jedidiah," she whispered, as if to explain it all.

I began to kneel up, but she pulled me back down. "No!" she pleaded. "I'm too embarrassed."

"Too embarrassed? Why?"

"Swear you won't tell? Swear? Cross your heart and hope to die?"

I crossed my heart.

"Bess sent him an anonymous letter telling him

there's someone here who's in love with him and I'm so embarrassed. I could kill her." She knelt and peered over the tops of the grasses, her hands on her knees. "And I saw at mail call that he got it. I saw it right in his hands. He hadn't read it yet though. Maybe he's read it by now."

She glanced over at me. "There was a letter for you, too. Did you get it? A green envelope like your grandmother sends. You weren't there. I think Jed took it for you."

Before she could stop me I burst from the grasses like a startled bird, flew up into the summer air, and sped across the field to where I could see Jedidiah walking away.

"Jedidiah! Jedidiah! Wait up!"

I saw it in his hand immediately and didn't even ask for it, just grabbed it and opened it on the spot. I read it out loud.

Dear Zoe, sweetheart,

I hope this letter finds you happy and enjoying yourself at camp. By the time you receive it, PopPop and I will be registered in a motel somewhere in

Boston. *As soon as we arrive and settle, I will call Jed's mother and give her our number in case of an emergency. Nothing to worry about really. It's just that something has come up suddenly, and, well, it's nothing for you to worry about.*

And don't concern yourself about Oscar. Mr. Gilroy has taken him for the week, and you know how Oscar loves him! I'm sure he will put on a few pounds before we see him again.

Please keep writing your letters. See you soon, sweetheart. I know you are having a wonderful time with Jed, but I look forward to having you back home again.

Love from PopPop too,
Grandma

I looked up at Jedidiah, stunned. "Boston? My grandparents went to Boston? What can they be doing there?"

Jed took the letter out of my hands and read it through himself. "That's weird. Do they have relatives there or anything?"

I shook my head. "PopPop has a brother in Alaska, and Grandma has a cousin in New York City, but Boston? No. Nobody."

I noticed Jed was studying me, looking at the scrape on the side of my face. When I glared at him he looked back down at the letter.

"They said I was sleepwalking," I told him.

His eyes were kind, soft, my old Jedidiah. "So I heard. Were you?"

"Don't believe it for a minute," I ordered him, and I began to walk faster, away from him.

"Then what happened?" He kept pace with me.

"I went home again."

I could sense his disbelief gleaming off him like a dim glow off roadside goldenrod, but I turned to face him. We stopped there in the field. "Jed, you have to believe me. You have to trust me and you have to do something for me."

"You are really scaring me, Zoe. What's going on?"

"Please just trust me for now, okay? And just one thing. Just one. This afternoon, at the volley-ball game, make an excuse for me. If anyone notices I'm not there, tell them I went into town with the cookie buyers, or that I'm at the nurse's. Anything. You'll know what to say."

"You're not leaving the camp, are you? You'll get in terrible trouble if you do, and so will I."

"I promise I won't even leave my cabin. How's that? You have my word. I just need some time alone there."

"In your cabin?"

"That's all."

He grew quiet and we began walking to the mess hall. "If it's that important to you. . . ."

"It's very important."

He handed back my grandmother's letter and I folded it and pressed it back in its green envelope. "Thanks, Jedidiah. You're the best."

He dropped back then, and I continued on alone through the grasses, the deep grasses, the low grasses, then the path. Paths are like that. Even if you try to avoid them, they crop up, appearing beneath your feet and you find yourself following them anyway. And my path, now that I had seen my mother with my grandparents, was suddenly and irrevocably to go to them.

Now I have never been a willful person. I couldn't ever remember stomping my foot or demanding my way. Zoe Louise, the ghost of my childhood, had made up for all that I lacked in stubbornness. So when I became so single-minded about seeing my mother again, I reminded myself of Zoe Louise. And I became like her in more ways than I like to admit.

SIX

There are not many places you can go to be alone at summer camp. Between the activities and the events, there is hardly a minute to have a thought of your own, unless you are like me. If you are a loner by nature, you will scout out all the private places, the hiding spots, that no one else notices.

The volleyball match began at two o'clock, and I ran back to my cabin with the excuse to get my wristband, nodding imperceptibly to Jedidiah as I trotted off in full view of everyone. No one called me back. No one asked.

The cabin was dark as I closed the door behind

me. I did not turn on the lights. I did not get my wristband. I stood in the middle of the room and let my eyes adjust to the shadowy stillness, the bunks pushed against the outer walls, the towels hung along the back wall, the shutters closed against the midday sun.

Looking up I could see the cool darkness of the eaves, and the opening in the low ceiling off to one side. There was no ladder to get up there, no chair. As quietly as I could, I pushed one of the beds so that it was right under the opening. Then, standing on the bed, bouncing softly as though on a trampoline, I grasped the edges of the opening—but then just hung there stupidly, my legs dangling and whipping around. I tumbled onto the bed. Then I pushed the bed over more, so that the metal headboard, higher than the mattress, was under the opening. I tried again. Bouncing, grasping the edges, and then stepping up on the headboard so that my head went up into the eaves. Carefully, steadily, I braced myself, and with one mighty lurch, flung myself up onto the floor of the eaves and pulled my legs up after me.

I stood crouched over. All around me our empty trunks were lined up, trunks that had carried all our possessions and had arrived at camp a couple of days before we had. Now they were all here, black, empty, and like me, waiting to go home.

I crept to the end of the eaves, to a small round window on the wall, and looked out. I could hear the volleyball game, the sudden whoops and shouts, and the whistle, but I couldn't see it. All I could see were the solid maple leaves, dense, undersea green leaves rustling outside the cabin. I pulled one of the trunks over to the window and sat on it, my face close to the window.

Only then did I begin to feel frightened. This was not something the counselors would have allowed me to do. And certainly Grandma, for all her gentleness and patience, would not have liked this. Perhaps only my mother. I thought how only my mother might have understood, approved, even called to me. So I closed my eyes, and feeling a light trembling in my chest, I listened for her voice.

Instantly, too soon, too suddenly, too hard, I began to feel heavy, like a giant hand was pressing me onto the trunk, pushing me down, crushing me. I fell over onto my side, the trunk catching me. I squeezed my eyes shut, bringing my clenched fists to my mouth, and I tried not to cry out. I concentrated on what I had to do—straining to hear my mother calling. Her child voice calling to me.

But instead—as if from the end of a long tunnel—

"Jessie, dear!"

It was my grandmother calling. And my mother's name. "Jessie, lunchtime!"

"Just a minute!" a child answered.

I experienced an odd tumbling motion, and then suddenly, as though I had been tossed from a great distance, I found myself teetering on the edge of my grandmother's vegetable garden. I stumbled to catch my balance, noticing instantly how cold everything was, dead and bare, bare stakes, wilted stalks; and whipping about the garden were dried leaves once more. The air stung with a crisp autumn wind.

A small child was crouched in the dirt, her face a picture of deep concentration, her small arms wrapped around a big orange pumpkin. "Too heavy," she muttered. "It got too big."

I wasn't sure she would be able to see me and I didn't know what to say. I stepped forward, into the dirt of the garden, and she looked up. Her face was simple and clean, so bright and rosy. My mother.

"It wasn't so heavy yesterday," she told me. "But it got bigger! Now it's too big. Way too big!"

She stood and clapped her hands together, not to clap off the dirt, but more because she had seen someone older do that. I guessed she was about five years old. "Maybe you'd better do it," she said simply.

I tried to speak. "What do you want me to do?"

"Take it over there." She pointed across the stretch of grass to the back stoop. "To surprise Mommy." It seemed far to me in my shadowy condition. I knew from experience it might feel like miles. But she was looking at me. "Well? What are you waiting for?" she finally asked.

"I'll try," I said.

I strained to remember what Zoe Louise had told me about touching things when you are a ghost, how you send your thoughts to your fingers and your hands, just like your heart sends blood there. And if you do it right, you will feel solid and real, even in this other time, and then you can actually touch something, even move it, eat it, smell it.

So I sent my thoughts to my hands, to the ends of my fingers and bent over the pumpkin. I could smell how orange it was. I could hear how heavy and thick it was. The child came close and I could see her breath curling about me.

"Got it?" she asked.

I didn't answer, but smoothed my hands over the hard surface, lost in the sensation; and then reaching all the way around the pumpkin, I lifted it easily.

"Oh! You're so strong!" the child cried, and she jumped about me. "Over here! Over here now!" and she danced across the grass to the back stoop. I began to laugh, joy welling up inside me like bubbles, for once I had lifted it, I found the pumpkin to be as light as air, like a paper Chinese ball.

Impulsively I held it above my head and danced also. I spun and turned and laughed and called her to watch me. The stretch of grass was easy—simple for me.

When I reached the back stoop, the back door opened suddenly and my grandmother was standing on the top step. "Jessie, your soup is getting cold, honey. Come on in now."

I froze, the pumpkin suspended in the air above my head.

"But my friend is bringing the pumpkin in."

"Is that right? Well, you can come back out again once you're done with lunch." I saw her look around the yard, as though for a friend, or a pumpkin, and knew she couldn't see me.

I stepped closer, letting the pumpkin drop in my arms, and I hugged it before me. My grandmother was beautiful—her skin smooth against her cheeks, her eyes clear and playful. Her neck that I knew to be soft and loose-skinned was long and thin disappearing into the collar of her woolen blouse. She held the door open with one arm and with her other arm she kept her sweater closed against her chest. I could see her arms were smooth and thin. She was my grandmother, but she was other than my grandmother. She was young, so young, yet even in this moment, with cool autumn winds blowing over her, she wore only socks on her feet—like always. I knew her shoes would be under the kitchen table, side by side.

"Then leave the pumpkin right here," the child was saying to me. She was looking straight into my eyes, seeing me. "Right here." She patted the bottom step and then ran up them into the house. I stood there stunned and watched as my grandmother smiled indulgently at her child and then closed the door behind them.

They were gone. Silence. The pumpkin and I stood invisibly at the bottom of the steps.

How sad I felt. I had had only a moment with my mother, and she had forgotten me so easily, by now sipping her soup, lost in her own time with her own mother. Gently I laid the pumpkin on the bottom step and stepped as quietly as I could up to the door. I peeked in through the curtain and saw them sitting at the table. My grandmother was wiping my mother's hands with the wet corner of a kitchen towel, and after she'd wiped her small face, she sat down at the table too, with her back toward me.

I was tempted to knock, to see if I could call my mother back to me. After all, when would I see her again? But suddenly and without warning, I realized someone had mounted the steps beside me. I turned and saw his face. He was a large man, heavy, and I could feel a sort of heat coming off him. I waited for him to knock, to call out to my grandmother and state his business, for clearly he did not see me standing there. But he didn't move. He just stood there, looking in at them. I didn't know why then, but the hair stood up along the base of my neck.

He drew closer to the window, forming two steamy circles with his stale breath. I stared at him—his heavy jowly face, his rough chin pressed low against his buttoned coat collar. His hands were thrust deep into his coat pockets and he seemed to sway very slowly from one foot to the other, never taking his eyes off the child inside.

"Who are you?" I said, and when he didn't hear or notice me, I said louder, "What do you want?" He rubbed the back of his hand across his nose and coughed softly. I could smell something bad, something very bad.

Inside my grandmother stood and moved to the sink. The man ducked quickly away from the window and as though he had created an undertow, I was pulled off the steps to land in the grass.

"What are you doing here?" I cried after him, but he didn't see me. He was intent on leaving the house, and he lumbered back toward the garden. He moved heavily but quickly, and I could sense there was a terrible, dangerous strength in his awkwardness. Then I watched horrified as he walked into the garden and lifted the big pumpkin. I spun around. Where was it? It wasn't on the step! Had I never brought it to the step at all? No, of course I had! My mother had seen me! Had danced beside me!

I watched as he lifted the pumpkin and came toward the house. Coming and coming. I could here his low voice rumbling, saying, "Gorman bring. Gorman bring the pumpkin." He struggled with the huge pumpkin.

I threw myself in front of him, to block him, to keep him away from the steps, but he passed through me like smoke through a porch screen, and silently, concentrating all his strength on being silent, he placed the pumpkin on the bottom step with a grunt. "Gorman do," he said.

"But I put it there!" I shouted. "I put it there! Not you! She'll know it wasn't you! It was me!"

But he didn't hear me. "Gorman do," he repeated in a voice that was almost too slow and too low to be heard. Backing away from the pumpkin, he turned and ran heavily into the woods.

SEVEN

*P*ut it where?"

"I put it on the back steps!"

"Put what on the back steps, Zoe? Wake up, stop it!" Jedidiah was crouching over me, his hands on my shoulders, shaking me gently, but steadily.

"The pumpkin, the pumpkin," I told him, and I started to cry when I realized I was back in my own time.

"What are you talking about?" he asked. "Zoe, you're not making any sense, none at all."

Not even caring what he might think, and between sobs, I sat up and told him. "I saw my mother, I actually saw her when she was very young."

"Your mother?" Jed sat on the trunk beside me. "You had a dream about her?"

"No, Jedidiah, I saw her for real. I saw her exactly as she was, years ago, when she was little and still happy. You know, before anything bad ever happened to her."

"You are not making any sense. You know that, don't you?"

"Oh, how can I make you understand? Can't you just believe me, because you know me? Believe me because I say so?"

He spoke evenly and deliberately. "Believe that you just saw your mother when she was little and that you put a pumpkin on the back steps." He paused. "Mmmmm—no. No. I can not."

All strength and persuasiveness went out of me. "Oh, I don't blame you," I whispered. "I don't blame you at all," and I started to cry again. I was never a crier, but there was something about coming back, about making the shift, that left me weak and vulnerable, wrung out. Resisting this over-whelming weakness, and having a sudden flash of terror, I thought of Gorman and cried, "Oh no!" bolting to my feet and cracking the side of my head on a low beam.

My head rang like a bell, my ears roared, and I pressed my fingers hard against a cut and a bump that pulsed under my hair. I felt Jedidiah lock his arms around me to hold me still. "Easy, girl, easy," he said softly. He didn't believe what I was telling him, but I could tell he knew that I believed it. And so he was soft with me, tender.

"There's a very bad man, Jedidiah." Not taking my hands away from my ringing head, I drew back and looked him in the eyes. I had to make him understand. "There's a terrible man there who is watching my mother, sneaking around, spying on her."

"Okay," he said. I could hear the disbelief in his voice.

"There *is*!"

"I said okay. Okay! What do you want me to do? I can't imagine what any of this means, Zoe. You're hardly making any sense!"

"I've gotta go back. I've gotta get to him before

he hurts her. I know he's going to hurt her."

Suddenly, from the other end of the eaves—

"What is going on here?"

I had never seen Amanda look so stern. Her face was pale, and her mouth a thin tense line. Just her upper body extended from the hole in the floor. And beside her, Danielle rose like a submarine gun to gloat at us.

"I knew they were here," Danielle said. "See?"

Amanda turned to her and seemed to yank her from sight. Then she turned back to glare at us. Barely moving her lips she said, "Get down, right this instant. I will meet you in the counselors' cabin in two minutes. You are in serious trouble." And she disappeared through the opening in the floor.

"Oh, Jedidiah, I'm sorry. Why did you come? Why didn't you just stay where you were?"

"I was worried. I don't like what you're doing. I feel responsible. I know the rules around here, and you can't do this, whatever it is." Jedidiah looked defeated.

"I'm sorry, Jed. I'm so sorry." He began to creep away from me. "But please—" I held his arm in a tight grip and our eyes met. He looked away. "Please don't tell them what I'm doing."

He breathed out and turned back to me. "How can I tell them when I have no idea what it is you're doing?" He flushed red and shook my hand off his arm. He began to yell at me. "What am I going to tell them, that you're moving pumpkins? Chasing bogeymen? Do me a favor, would you?" He had never yelled at me before, not ever.

I looked at my bloody fingers. Felt my hair, which was sopping wet now. Worse, worst of all, was hearing him yell at me. "What?" I whispered.

"Don't tell me any more about it. Okay? And don't ask me to help you. That's it. Don't ask again."

"Okay," I agreed, but I don't think he heard me. He had disappeared down the hole in the floor leaving me there. I felt like I was losing everything.

When I walked cautiously into the counselors' cabin I was surprised to see a man I'd never seen before. He didn't say anything, but just sort of hung in the background. Monty and Amanda did all the talking.

"What did you two think you were doing?" Monty began when I sat down beside Jedidiah in a folding chair.

Neither of us answered. Amanda walked up to me brusquely and without any warmth or tenderness, picked through my sticky hair to examine my cut.

"Stitches?" asked Monty.

"No. I don't think so. Just superficial," she answered.

"Lucky," Monty muttered. "Jed. What about you? What were you doing in the girls' cabin? You know you don't belong there."

"Looking for Zoe," Jed answered. "She's been acting weird, and . . ." I could feel him squirming in his seat. "I don't know. I just had a bad feeling. I wanted to find her. You know. Make sure she was okay."

"It didn't occur to you to tell me or Amanda that you were worried and that Zoe had disappeared?"

"No, sir."

"Why not?"

"Well, actually, Zoe had asked me not to tell anyone. Said she had to do something. That she needed time alone in her cabin. And it was real important."

Amanda held an ice pack out before me and I took it, lowered my head, and pressed it against my bump.

"Zoe?" Monty said.

I began slowly. "Well, I was going to play volleyball, but I thought I might need my wristband so I went back to the cabin to get it. And I couldn't find it, so I thought it might be in my trunk still, so—"

I could feel Jedidiah glaring at me.

I could feel my voice getting smaller and smaller. I was not a good liar. My nerve abandoned me. And I became silent.

"I can't believe that," said a man's voice. The stranger in the room left the back wall and came to stand in front of me. I looked up at him and then ducked my head back down, pressing the cold ice pack to my bump. "Tell me something, Zoe. I know this has been your first year here."

67

"Who are you?" I asked trembling. I glanced at Amanda, uncertain.

"Hank Reynolds," he answered. "I own Camp Cedar Ravine. I've owned it for twenty-seven years, and we've never had any serious discipline problems in all those years.

"And you see, Zoe, you are as new to us as we are to you. We don't know each other very well and we're wondering . . ." He turned and walked toward the windows. "Are you aware that all the campers have to put their valuables, their radios, their cash, et cetera, in a safe in the main building, and that those trunks are all empty?"

I gasped. "No!" I said, too loud, too sudden. "I mean, no I didn't know that, but that's not why I was—"

Jed piped in—"Zoe would never—"

"Quiet!" Mr. Reynolds snapped and turned back to us. We couldn't help staring back at him.

"I wasn't stealing," I said with all the openness of a cracked egg. I felt like I was leaking out all over the floor.

"Then you tell me what was going on. What else

are we to think? Tell me why two young people—a boy and a girl—were hiding away? What were you doing up there? What were you planning to do?"

I looked over at Amanda and Monty in time to see them exchange a glance. This had taken a turn I couldn't believe, and I could tell they were equally shocked. I looked at Jedidiah. His ears were flame red and his eyes were brimming over with embarrassed tears.

"I've heard that you two seem to have an unnaturally close relationship—"

"Not *unnaturally*, Mr. Reynolds," cut in Amanda. "Just unusual. They are old friends, known each other a long time, and we just thought that . . . It isn't really necessary to . . ."

Mr. Reynolds's voice was loud and cold. "I think it would be safe to say that two thirteen-year-olds of opposite sexes are not your natural selection of best-friend possibilities. That is, unless one or both is a little precocious, and something else is going on."

"It wasn't like that," Jedidiah said.

"Well, there's really no way we can tell now, is there?"

I hung my head. How could this have happened?

"So this is what we will do," Mr. Reynolds said. He wove his fingers together like a hard basket and paced slowly in front of us. "If we weren't at the end of the camp session anyway, I would have called for your parents"—he looked particularly at me—"excuse me, your *grandparents*, to come get you. But it's Friday, and we'll all be leaving tomorrow. I understand your grandparents are in Boston as we speak, preparing to pick you up on their way home."

My head snapped around to look at Amanda and she met my eyes. "Your grandmother called just a little while ago. Right after she had called Mrs. Seger," she explained. "That's why I came looking for you."

"So, the rule young lady, for the rest of your stay, is to buddy up—not with Jedidiah—and you are not to leave that buddy's side until you are in your grandparents' car heading out of here. Is that clear?"

Even as he spoke, I knew he couldn't keep me. I trembled with the sudden knowledge that it wasn't the place, the camp, that they would fail to trap me in; it was the moment, the time. I knew clearly for the first time that like Zoe Louise, I was no prisoner of any age or year, and that somehow I would find a way to return to my mother again.

I looked up at him defiantly and met his stare. The trembling in my body had stopped. *Think that I am a thief,* I silently dared him. *Go ahead. You don't know anything.*

He frowned and looked away. "Jedidiah. You should know better. This is your seventh year here. And we will discuss this with your parents when they come. You're excused."

Jed burst from his chair like a trapped animal and bolted out the door. Amanda stepped forward. "Mr. Reynolds, I told her grandmother Zoe would call her right back." I saw Amanda look at the man nervously. Like me, she knew he had gone too far.

"Let her call," he said, and he didn't bother to look at me again. He gathered up some papers while Amanda motioned me to her. I sat in the chair by her desk, and she dialed a number that was on her pad. She handed it to me as it rang.

"Hello?"

"Grandma?" I almost wept at the sound of her voice.

"Honey! What's the matter? I called Jedidiah's mom to tell her where we were and she said you were terribly upset."

I heard my voice like a whining child's. "I didn't know where you were. I didn't get your letter till this morning."

"Well, I'm sorry, honey. Mrs. Seger told me what happened, and I had no idea that you would try to reach us—"

Around me, I could sense everyone leaving. Mr. Reynolds had packed up his papers and put them in a case, and he was walking with Monty to the door. They talked quietly to each other and left. Amanda was there, and then when I looked for her, she wasn't. She must have stepped into the other room.

I held the phone tightly to my ear. I whispered, "Grandma. Grandma."

"What, honey?" Her voice was still, waiting.

"Grandma. Who was Gorman?"

And then I felt her silence, felt her drop away from me as though I were flying low over a stretch of prairie only to have the ground drop away into a canyon that echoed endlessly beneath me.

"Grandma?"

EIGHT

*F*inally my grandmother spoke. "Why?" Her voice was small. "Why are you asking that?"

"I . . . I . . . had a dream," I lied. "A dream about a man named Gorman and my mother."

"That is so strange," she said softly. "So strange that you would dream that now."

"Who was he?" I insisted.

"A man," she said hesitantly. "A man that lived near us years ago, down in the house by the ferry. He lived with his old mother. They were very odd, peculiar . . . very terrible."

I heard my grandfather's inquiring voice in the

background and my grandmother said, "Zoe had a dream about Gorman."

"My God," I heard him say and I couldn't exactly hear it, but I knew my grandmother had begun to cry. My grandfather took the phone.

"Zoe?"

"PopPop! What's going on? Where are you? Why are you in Boston? Why aren't you home?"

"It's a very long story, Zoe, but your mother is in a hospital here, and the doctors thought it would be helpful if Grandma and I came to see her, and to talk to them about your mother's childhood. About whatever we know."

"Mom? In a hospital?" That possibility hadn't even occurred to me. "What's wrong? What is it?"

PopPop's voice became slow, even, as though to calm me or to calm himself. "She had some sort of breakdown, Zoe. Actually it was a while ago. And she needs us right now. She's feeling stronger already. We'll stay with her another day and then we are coming to get you. Then we'll go home."

"Will she be all right?"

"We hope so," he said. "The doctors think so."

"Did Gorman hurt her?" I blurted out. "Did he do something to hurt her?"

"What are you talking about, Zoe? What do you know about Gorman?"

"He's a very bad man, PopPop. I feel so scared."

"Shhhh, honey," PopPop whispered gently. "It was long ago, so long ago. Why would you be scared?"

I felt an arm go around my shoulders and looked up to see Amanda beside me. She was frowning at my crusted hair, the sternness in her eyes now softened with something I wasn't sure of, was it worry? "Tell them you'll see them tomorrow," she whispered. She held me in her gaze and nodded at me.

"I'd better go, PopPop. I gotta go. You're going to come for me yourself? Are you sure it's okay? I won't be going home with Jed's parents?"

"That's right, sugar. We thought we'd take a little drive to get you."

"It's a long drive, PopPop."

"Not too long to have you with us again."

"You sure?"

"Have we ever let you down?" he asked.

"Never," I answered. And because I couldn't bare to hang on another minute and because I couldn't bare to say good-bye, I hung up the phone without a sound. I wouldn't cry in front of Amanda.

"Go wash up and I'll meet you at dinner," Amanda said. She sounded softer. "We'll get you a buddy starting then, okay?"

I didn't answer. I knew it wasn't her fault, but I couldn't talk to her anymore.

Now imagine this. Imagine that you learn to play a piece of music on a harmonica, from beginning to end, an entire song. That's what ghost-walking was like for me, something I was mastering. Now imagine that even though you can play a whole song, every once in a while you play just a single note, just for the sheer sound of it, the clear vibration in the air. That's also what was beginning to happen. I didn't need to leave my body completely, didn't need to have a total experience: I could do it just a little.

That night Amanda appointed Leah to be my buddy. Told us we were to stay shoulder to shoulder, hip to hip, until, as Mr. Reynolds had said, I was in my "grandparents' car headed out of here." It seemed an unfair burden to place on Leah, to be my jailer and keeper, but I think she was chosen because she was an agreeable girl who never seemed to have any of her own urges. She always went along gladly, no problem. The difficult part about Leah for me was that she was Danielle's best friend.

I brought my tray silently to the dinner table and sat beside Leah with Danielle opposite us. It hadn't taken me long to realize that Danielle believed I had stolen Jedidiah away from her. I knew by her steely looks that she took what had happened between Jedidiah and me personally, as though I had somehow betrayed her.

So Danielle and Leah sat there talking, acting as though I wasn't at the table at all. Actually I *was* beginning to leave my body just a little—a harmonica note blown clear and pure into the air. At first I pulsed in and out of my body, and then I began to sway, like swinging easy on an old swing. Just soft and easy, back and forth, holding on to the present as I would hold on to the heavy rope of the swing, feeling the hard seat beneath me, yet sensing the emptiness dropping out from under my feet. I looked across the room for Jedidiah, to see if he could see it happening, but he sat with his back to me. I wondered if I could leave, slip out of my body while I was in their midst. Maybe go to him.

Then I lifted my arm, but I didn't really lift my arm. I lifted it so anyone looking would see the fork go to my lips, but I knew my hand was in my lap at the same time. Then I left my hands in front of me folded on the table, and with a part of me that could not be seen, I reached across Leah's back and tugged steadily at a single strand of her long hair, pull, pull, feeling the fiber of her hair stretch and lengthen, and then suddenly she scratched her head and shook out her hair absentmindedly.

I was groggy with amazement at myself. I believed I could have left them right then. I could have shot up into the sky and been gone. I think. I wasn't sure. I was skitterish, shaky, not knowing what I could trust about myself and what I couldn't. I longed to be home again, to be at the kitchen table safe between my two grandparents. Yet I knew there was something I had to do that was more pressing than anything I had ever done in my life. So with no one able to see what was happening, I stood poised, like a diver on a high board, bouncing, slowly bouncing. . . .

In our cabins that night we discovered our trunks had been brought down and placed at the foot of our beds. All our paintings, our posters and hangings, were stripped from the walls and tossed on the beds to be sorted out and packed away. We were told to start packing our things, in preparation for our return home. But spirits were high. And I quickly realized a sort of euphoria had taken over. It was intense, everyone promising to write through the winter, making vows, swearing eternal friendship, signing one another's sheets with bright-red markers, trading sweatshirts, sitting on one another's beds with arms linked, combing one another's hair.

I pretended I wasn't watching. Maybe once it would have been possible for me to be at least on the fringes of such friendliness. But now, it felt as though everyone was mad at me. Angry people were piling up around me like darts around a dart board. If these girls had once thought they understood my friendship with Jedidiah, they no longer did. And now they were aloof from me, distant. Maybe I even flatter myself to think they were angry at me. The fact was, they ignored me.

I tucked everything that was on my bed in a roll and tossed it into my trunk. Without changing into my nightshirt, or taking off my sneakers, I unzipped my sleeping bag and slid into it. I punched the pillow hard and dropped my head into the dent. The room grew suddenly silent.

"You okay, Zoe?"

It was Leah, my watchdog, my jailer. I didn't answer. I heard footsteps across the floor planks and I shut my eyes quick. I could feel her standing right in front of me. She was silent for a moment, and then I heard the others snicker, giggle among themselves.

"So be like that," she said, with a hint of Danielle's snotty voice. And she went away. I didn't move. I didn't brush away the tears that spilled from my eyes and seeped into my pillow. They all had mothers. In a couple of days I would see them all, the mothers and fathers getting out of their station wagons and cars, hugging their daughters and their sons. I had seen them that first day when all the kids were dropped off. I had stepped out of Jedidiah's parents' car with him and stretched and looked around me warily. Jedidiah's mother had known, known my heart, because before they drove away, she had pulled me to her and hugged me hard, startling us both, I think. "You'll be fine, Zoe," she had said.

And now tomorrow, my grandparents would be coming for me. The kids would all see Grandma in her flowered dress, and PopPop in—oh, in his old red truck. They would have to drive the truck up to get me. The same truck they had most likely used to go visit my mother in the hospital. I felt as though a wide chasm was opening, ready to swallow me up, on one side my love for the two old people who loved me and knew me best, and on the other my foolish shame, to have everyone know they were all I had. No mother to be seen.

I pulled the pillow in front of me and hugged it furiously, holding back my sobs, and then all voices ceased. All laughter disappeared and I felt as though a trapdoor opened beneath me. Great creaking hinges swung down and dropped me into blackness.

NINE

A small hand was stroking my head. Gently. Silently. I woke with that awful startled sense of being dropped from a high place, and my whole body shuddered.

"Shh, shhh," she whispered patting me, stroking me. "Don't be afraid now. Don't cry."

I opened my eyes wide. It was cold in the room and a small doll blanket was covering my bare arm. I rolled onto my back. My mother, the little child, was sitting beside me on the small bed PopPop had once built for her. We were in the playhouse, the old miniature house he had fixed up for me years ago when I had first come to live with them. Of course, it had been my mother's first.

Through the small archway I could see the table and chairs in the center of the main room, and a child-size sink and stove beneath the window. Without looking, I knew that each burner was painted with a bright-red flame for making tea and oatmeal and a pretend Sunday dinner.

I looked back at the child beside me. She was wearing a little red corduroy jacket with a plaid hood. Cradled in her arms was a wooden doll with wiry yellow hair and a painted-on smile. "Feeling better now?" she asked me. Without waiting for an answer she said, "This is my baby and you're my big girl and as soon as we have lunch we're all going to the circus. Here." She tucked a cracker into my hand, and not knowing whether or not the cracker would fall through my fingers, I took it. It held. I didn't dare put it to my mouth. She sat there thoughtfully munching on her own cracker, and once in a while she'd hold it to her doll's mouth.

"Now some tea," she ordered, and she got up and stood by the side of the bed looking at me. "I'll set the table and boil the water. Don't forget to brush your teeth and put your blue dress on, the one with the birds." She left me lying there, and I could hear her at the stove, making tea-making noises and talking to her doll whom she had put at the table. Slowly I unwound my body from its cramped bed. I sat up and dropped my feet to the floor. I knew the bright linoleum beneath my feet. I knew its little dots and patterns. How often I had sat on it myself, rocking my dolls to sleep, and playing with my then-ghostly friend. Zoe Louise had used to like to sweep the floor with the little broom after she had trailed in a bunch of leaves and grass.

It was quiet in the little house, and still. There was only the sound of a little girl making a pot of tea, but as I forced myself to stand, other sounds swirled in my head, making me dizzy and uncertain.

"Leah! Watch this. I can put it here. Watch, watch. Do this. Fold it like this."

"Like this? Like this?"

I could hear Leah, Danielle. They were laughing, helping each other pack. I shook my head and willed them to be quiet. And like a twitch that is

86

rubbed hard and deep, it was gone. I walked out of the little alcove and went to my mother. I sat at her little table and studied her.

I have often wondered how I knew this was my mother, and as I sat there I wondered it even then. I was so sure it was her, so absolutely positive, but I needed to find something concrete, something exactly common between my mother then and my mother now, something real I could point to. Her back was to me, and her arms and her legs were pudgy and pale, and there was nothing about them that was familiar to me. They were like the arms and legs of every little girl I had ever known.

She turned then and came toward me carrying a teapot in one hand and a tiny cup and saucer in the other. She placed the cup and saucer before me and poured, making a funny *plp, plp, plp* sound with her lips. I watched her face and smiled. Yes, the mouth. "Be careful now," she said to me. "It's very, very hot. Blow on it."

I didn't move. "Are you awake?" she asked. She peered into my eyes. Yes, the eyes. And I knew her eyes.

"Do this," I told her, and I covered my hand over the lower half of my face. She imitated me, and I studied her eyes, her eyebrows, her wispy hairline. Yes, that was my mother, too.

"Now do this," I said, and I covered the upper part of my face with my hand. She did this too, and I recognized her chin, the set of her jaw.

"Simon says do this," she countered, and she put both hands over her ears. I did as she said.

"Simon says do this," and she put both hands in the air.

"Do this," and I followed with my hands to my knees as she had done, and she giggled wildly. "I win. I didn't say Simon. And Simon likes you to say Simon."

Her laughter was so startling to me, so infectious.

"Zoe says do this," I declared and I stood on the chair. She did the same, asking, "Zoe? Who's Zoe?"

"Me! I'm Zoe! Now Zoe says do this." I jumped off the chair. She did likewise. "Do this!" I spun around and around and she did too.

"Aha!" I said freezing in place. "I didn't say Zoe says."

She pretended she was trying to stop, laughing and spinning until she fell in a heap on the floor. She lay back on the floor and spread herself like a star. "I am so dizzy," she laughed. "Everything is rocking. Come see."

I lay down beside her and while she looked up at the ceiling, I looked at her, memorized her small profile. "Do you know me?" I asked softly.

She turned to meet my gaze. Her little hood almost covered her one eye, but she studied me. "You're my big girl," she answered. "You're my Zoe."

"Zoe! Zoe! There's a campfire! Come on! Let's go!"

"Come on. Down at the lake."

Then there was a single rap at the door. So abrupt and singular, that I wasn't sure I had heard it at all. It seemed a million sounds were calling for my attention, a million different moments tugging at me.

But my mother sat up. "Who's there?"

The door clicked, then slowly opened into the room. The doorway was blocked by a rough brown coat, and hanging from the sleeves were two long hands, dirty wrists, scraped knuckles. The coat was swelling, buckling, swelling, buckling with hard breathing, and then Gorman lowered his head and peered into the little house.

Someone was shaking me, shaking me.

"Come on, Zoe. We're not going to baby-sit you here. You have to come down to the lake. That's all there is to it. I don't care how tired you are. It's not fair to Leah that she miss last campfire because of you."

Danielle was standing beside my bed with her hands on her hips. Leah was beside her, frowning.

I didn't dare speak. Surely if I had said a word it would have broken my tie with my mother, with my moment in the little house. Stunned, shaken, I sat up and looked down at my hands. Faintly I thought I could see my bones glowing through the flesh of my fingers. I looked down at my feet and saw the wood grain through the transparent bubbles of my toes. I glanced up at Danielle and Leah and realized it was dim at my end of the room and they couldn't see what was happening to me. Then without muttering a single word, I stood before them, face to face, expressionless, barely breathing.

Danielle and Leah glanced at each other. "Weird," Danielle said softly. "I can't believe this." They shook their heads and walked away from me, their arms locked.

"Come with us now to the campfire," Leah ordered, and I obeyed. I followed them out the door, as though I were walking across a frozen lake trying not to break through the ice. But I knew I had to get back to my mother. And somehow I knew I had to stay with her for as long as I could.

All around me, I could smell Gorman. Gorman sweating. Gorman breathing hard.

TEN

We joined the ranks of all the kids heading down to the lake. A dusky light filtered through the trees as Danielle and Leah walked ahead of me, turning now and then to check that I was still there. I kept my eyes on the ground, and then I slowed. "I'm going to faint again," I whispered and they both stopped to face me.

"Aw, come on, Zoe, don't do that. We don't want to stay here now. We want to go down to the lake. There's supposed to be a surprise."

"Go ahead without me. I'll be there in a minute." The smell. The smell. I could barely breathe. I sat on the side of the path and wrapped my arms around myself, my disappearing hands tucked out of sight under the sleeves of my sweatshirt. I kept my head down. I rocked gently. "Go ahead. I'll be all right." I could hear the other campers passing, passing silently as they approached, stopping their conversations and looking at me.

Danielle asked one of them, "Where's Amanda? Is she on her way?"

The walkers kept walking and called behind them, "She's already down at the lake. All the counselors are there already. They want us to hurry." And they were gone.

"Zoe," Leah moaned. "You're making us miss—"

Then there were more footsteps and these slowed and came to a halt before me. "Zoe? What's wrong?"

It was Jedidiah.

"She thinks she's going to faint again." Danielle's voice was icy, mean. "Although who can believe a word she says."

He crouched beside me. "You okay?" His hand was on my shoulder.

I shook my head no, and I could hear one of the girls actually stamp her foot on the path. "This isn't fair," she whined. "It's not fair that we have to stay behind because of her."

"You want me to stay with you?" he whispered close to my ear.

"You'll get in trouble," I said without looking at him.

He stood and spoke to the girls. "Go on ahead," he said. "I'll wait until she feels she can walk and then I'll bring her on down to the shore. I'll look for you. I'll bring her right to wherever you are. Save her a spot."

I could hear Danielle and Leah hesitate. I imagined them looking at each other, thinking, What could be the harm? It's the last night. Could we really get into trouble now?

"All right," Danielle said. "We'll be by the lifeguard chair. Look for us there."

"Got it," Jed said agreeably, and I heard them run off. As soon as their footsteps faded I bolted up and ducked into the trees at the side of the path.

"Zoe! What are you—" Jed came after me and I

ran and ran until I got to a clearing, a clearing that was bright, where there was still some daylight heavy above us. I turned and I faced him. Held out my arms in front of me, palms down.

"Look at my hands, Jed," I ordered softly.

He did, and I watched his face. He must have thought it was a trick of light, an illusion of sunset, because he held his hands beside mine, to see if his too looked transparent and flimsy in the light, but his hands were tan and strong, nails real and hard, and my hands were as delicate as the jellyfish we used to watch floating besides PopPop's skiff.

"Hold my hands, now," I said. He did. "Squeeze them," and his hand closed over mine and clamped shut into a fist as though mine weren't even there.

"What is this?" he demanded jumping backward away from me, his fingers opening in shock. "What's happening to you?"

"Can I trust you, Jedidiah? Can you be my friend, no matter what? Can you remember that no matter what happens, it's still me, Zoe, from school, your old island friend?"

"I think I can," he whispered flatly. "I could try."

"Jed, I'm passing in and out of another time and I need to find a place where I can be alone for a while, where no one will find me. A place where I can leave, where I can pass through time and not be called back." I started to pace around the small clearing. "I keep getting called back and back, and it's never the right time."

I tried to explain. "I don't expect you to understand, Jed. I don't know myself exactly what's happening so I can't explain it. I just know I have to be alone, somewhere safe, where no one knows where I am. Where no one can find me and force me back."

Jed was staring at me, clearly on the cusp of trust and utter disbelief. To win him over, I found myself playing that one long harmonica note, that one trick. Without moving I turned around inside my body, fully, again and again. My arms left the shell of my arms, my nose slipped from its case, my hair passed in front of my eyes. I was like a little paper umbrella twirling in his hand. I spun for Jedidiah until he begged me to stop.

Then, breathless, I heard him say, "Come. Come

quickly. I can take you out to the other side of the lake. No one will find you there." And together we ran from the clearing, across the path, to find the place where the canoes waited silently on a bed of pebbles.

Some evenings feel evil, when light comes not from a ball of late-day sun but from an enveloping gray that hovers over everything, like a dirty old glove. This evening was like that as Jedidiah and I made our way furtively down to the water. Our footsteps seemed to echo down off the canopy of trees, making us feel as though we were being followed, and an unsteady breeze pulled at our clothes. In the distance a crow called out, and I shivered.

With no one around to see us, I slipped one of my disappearing hands into Jedidiah's and though I felt a tremor pass through him, he let me. With my other hand I grasped his wrist as firmly as I could.

"Like Hansel and Gretel," I whispered.

He glanced back at me and I saw how worried he was. "Only you don't have pebbles in your pocket to find your way back, Zoe."

"Oh, yes, I do."

His eyes bore into mine.

"I do, I do. I will find my way back. I always do. It's like a rubber band pulling me back every minute while I am away. I can't *not* come back."

He continued on, holding my hand so tight that sometimes, my hand disappeared and we had to start again. If only the moon would come out, I thought. If the moon suddenly broke through the grayness, its light might have carried us like the memory of moonlight in my grandmother's dining-room window, the way it would illuminate the pale curtains and spill comfort onto everything. But the dirty glove pressed down on us. There was no memory to escape to. *This* was the memory.

ELEVEN

We could barely make out the low outline of the canoes along the cove's shoreline. We could hear the voices of the campers off to the right, through the stand of trees that sheltered the cove. Now, growing even more cautious, we crept along, willing the pebbles to be silent as we scattered them beneath our feet.

Jedidiah led the way to the farthest canoe. It was dark blue and nearly invisible. He motioned me to help him turn it right side up and lift it, rather than drag it into the water, but when I grabbed the edge it slipped through my fingers as though it were made of butter. My hands were no longer bone and muscles; they were more memory than reality. I was fading.

"Grab it!" Jed hissed. "Help me!"

"I can't," I whispered back. "My hands can't grip. I'm disappearing."

"Oh, God, Zoe," Jed sobbed. "I hope you know what you're doing. I hope to God you know." And slowly, but with great effort, he turned the canoe right side up, and then with a steady strength he began to push it alone toward the water. I followed, helpless, powerless. We could hear Monty's voice through the trees, singing, his ukulele pulled out for this special last night campfire. I could just make out his words—

"Daisy, Daisy, give me your answer true.

I'm half crazy, all for the love of you."

The lyrics seemed strangely sad to me. "Jedidiah," I whispered, but he ignored me.

"It won't be a stylish marriage

I can't afford a carriage."

Jedidiah placed two paddles in the canoe and then slid it silently into the water. In unison the two of us stepped into the canoe and we glided out into the shimmering darkness.

"But you'll look sweet
   Upon the seat——"

And when the paddle slipped through my fingers like warm sand, I abandoned it, knelt on the floor of the canoe and simply pressed my body against Jedidiah's strong back. He paddled hard and silent, away from the campsite, the paddle splaying pearls into the dark water, and the soft music disappearing totally into the thickness of the trees; and then as we rounded the bend, Monty's sweet song reached us so clearly across the water. It's funny what trees and water can do. Funny that we could be paddling away from the others and yet hear them as though they were right beside us.

And isn't time like that? We walk around bends of time, leaving someone behind, someone singing a song we love, and as they fade into the distance so does the song. And only later, we meet someone else on the trail, someone singing the same song, and there can come that clear moment, like the world through a soap bubble, when it all comes back, all memory, all recollection.

I am in my grandmother's house in the late afternoon, and she is rinsing string beans in the kitchen sink, touching the back of her wet hand to her brow to push her hair from her youthful face. She is singing, "*Daisy, Daisy, give me your answer true.*"

And I am invisibly behind her, pressed up against her warmth, tears streaming down my face, and with her I sing, "*I'm half crazy, all for the love——*"

But when I open my eyes I see——like a rifle sight along her shoulder——out the back door and down the steps. I see the autumn trees in dull November light, light that would be dark but for the sharp yellow of the maple leaves, and I see Gorman moving through the yard, his back to me, his shoulders hunched, his heavy loping gait. He is running, moving faster than he has any right to, too fast, and beside him is a little child, my mother, jabbering, kicking leaves, with her tiny trusting hand in his.

I must have called out. I must have shouted. Because suddenly the canoe is churning and Jedidiah has me pinned to its floor, his hand hard over my mouth and nose. I can't breathe. I struggle against him, crying, scrambling, but he is right on top of me.

"Shhhh," he hisses. "Zoe, what are you doing? Are you crazy? Shut up! Shut up!" He squeezes my face hard and then lets go, his hand poised over me, ready to smother me again.

"Hurry, Jed, oh, hurry, Jed. Before it's too late."

I see his face, close to me, peering over the edge of the canoe. "If they haven't heard you, idiot!" he whispers harshly. He waits. We float endlessly and there are no sounds. Only faint ukulele notes reach us. Angrily Jedidiah goes back to his seat and starts to paddle again. "Just stay there. Stay right there," he orders.

And I roll onto my side with my eyes closed and my ear pressed against the inner hull of our small boat. I listen to the water rushing past, feeling time run out.

Then a scraping startles me. We have reached the other side, but when I go to press my hand into the hull to lift myself, my hand slips through as through a crust of snow that gives way at the slightest touch, and I am instantly drenched. Jedidiah doesn't see this and I don't tell him. But he cannot help but see when he stands and reaches out to help me that I cannot stand on the seat of the canoe or on the edge anymore. What seem to be my legs splash through to the rough pebble beach. My shoes drop away like shredded flower petals. I no longer have feet.

"I'll come back for you—" he begins, but I tell him no.

"Please don't, Jed. You might come at the wrong moment, before I am done. You could ruin everything."

He hesitates, his familiar face twisted into a troubled frown. "How will you get back?"

I stare at the distant shore, see the glow of the campfire through the trees. How can I explain it when I do not understand it myself? So I say, "And how will you walk into tomorrow morning? How do any of us get anywhere?"

"Zoe," he says, as though to command something of me, but there is nothing left to say.

"Thank you, Jedidiah. You are a good friend." And I leave him there on the shore. I don't watch him paddle back. I don't wave. I don't say good-bye. I turn and run into the woods on this side, feeling like a chrysalis must feel when it is changing, turning, feeling as though I must be dying.

The wind rushes over my ears as I run and run and run. I feel my feet tear through the underbrush, tripping through twisted vines and fallen trees, but nothing stops me. I don't even know where I am going, but I know I must get there quickly. I hear my footsteps thudding through the coming night. Branches skim across my face, tangle in my hair, leaving no mark. Only my breath echoes all around me, and my heart pounds in the hollow of my ears.

Then I hear another nearby. I hear someone running alongside me, running, running. A little hand slips into mine and then out. I look and I am running beside my mother and Gorman. We are on the island and we are running through the woods, autumn leaves churning in the air around us, and I can tell by the slant of the earth that we are heading down to the ferry dock. My mother's steps are small, precise, and she is talking all the while.

"And my Daddy is down by the boat? My Daddy needs me to go fishing?" she is saying.

"He is waiting," Gorman says. I look at him and see him clearly. There's crust around his lips, and his hair is greasy and flat against his stained neck. His eyes are lidded, and my whole body shudders like a crow caught in a knot of vines as he looks down at her trotting beside him.

"Leave her be," I demand through clenched teeth, but he doesn't see me or hear me. I am in neither world. I am gone from the shore with Jedidiah. And I am not yet here.

"Jessie," I whisper to her, and I swoop low, like a barn swallow, touching her ear, weaving my fingers in her curls. "Jessie, go back home," I plead, but if she hears me she doesn't let on.

"Daddy loves to fish," she is saying. "*We* have a boat. You know that? Did you know that my Daddy has a boat?"

"Today it's Gorman's boat," he says simply, and

106

I rush ahead of them, to block their way. I am running backward, hovering, scampering, and suddenly they *whoosh* through me, undisturbed.

"Jessie!" I plead, but she says, "I can catch a big fish, right? I can get a really big fish."

She suddenly stops there on the path and holds her hands apart to show him how big, but he does not want to stop, and like an owl swooping down to snatch up a mouse by the scruff of its neck, he grabs the little hood on the back of her corduroy coat and lifts her in the air beside him as though she were weightless. He doesn't miss a step, and she begins to whimper.

"Wait, wait. Put me down," she cries, and so that my mother won't be hurt, so that the coat doesn't cut into her neck and choke her, I find myself holding her up in my arms, lifting her, running and running beside them, down to the ferry dock. Helping Gorman carry my mother to the ferry dock.

TWELVE

Once in a while, a sunset at the old ferry dock is stupendous, like no other light show in the entire world. The town's fishermen and clammers, hands rough and raw from the cold, finish up beneath its canopy, and tell themselves this is their day's true reward as they stow their gear and motor toward home. The cosmic oranges and pinks weave round one another like dancing children, and the blue sky turns deep lavender, then purple. So bright, so bright, almost noisy, even a blind person would know something was happening. And if someone were reading a newspaper on the dock or ferry, he would look up suddenly as though he heard someone calling.

Gorman stole my mother on just such a night.

Off to the side of the ferry dock's sloping bank, in brambles and muck, Gorman has stowed an old metal boat, a boat whose floor buckles and snaps as he pulls it toward the water. It is filled with broken clamshells, a dead fish; and my eye is instantly caught by an oddly familiar small starfish.

Gorman doesn't slow down. He tosses the child in as though she weighs no more than a sack of onions that he will collect later. Her sobs penetrate me like icy rain, and feeling the cold for the first time, I encircle her the best I can, trying to cover her with my ghostly body and my invisible arms.

Gorman walks the boat out into the water a ways, up past his knees in icy water, and then he hoists himself in. Before the boat rights itself, a wave of water overflows, dangerously, quickly, and then it stops. He sits himself on the seat in the middle of the boat and points to the place between his feet. "Sit here," he orders, and my mother, my small mother, her face wet from crying, her neck red from the tightness of her collar, pushes her bottom lip out and shakes her head no, as though she will take no more.

Gorman seems to ignore her, and fitting two old rotting oars into the battered green oarlocks, he begins rowing out into the bay. *To where? To where?* I wonder. Then without missing a beat of his steady rowing, he lifts a large heavy foot. His one foot alone must weigh as much as one of PopPop's large sacks of compost, and with it he shoves my mother to where he wants her to sit. Then, never taking his eyes off her, he just rows, steady, grim.

I see the land slip away from us. There is an uneasy choppiness to the water, the sunset, the current. The cold water laps cruelly against the side of the metal boat and sometimes comes over the top, sloshing around Gorman's feet. Drenching my mother. She shivers, oblivious to my presence.

Darkness is descending on the water, turning everything into purple silhouettes. In the distance I can see the ferry leaving the island, dragging slowing across the bay. And suddenly from it, a voice calling.

"Gorman! What are you doing, Gorman? You can't go out now!" A man's voice spills out across the water from the ferry. I can see no man, no person standing and calling. It is as though the ferry itself is calling Gorman back.

"Goin' fishin'," Gorman roars back, too loud, too deep.

My mother starts to cry, high-pitched and cranky. "No you're not! You're not fishing! I wanna go home. I want—"

The oars stop midstroke, and Gorman lets go of one of them, reaching to press my mother's face down into the floor of his boat.

"It's too choppy, Gorman!" the ferry calls. "Get back to the shore! Right now!"

"Yeah. Yeah," he says, not too loudly. "Yeah. Yeah."

My mother whimpers from between his feet.

So this is the bad thing. This is the bad thing that happened so long ago. Rigid with rage and terror, I find myself pacing the perimeter of the boat, its very rim, sharp and hard, stepping fiercely along the rusted gunwale like a seagull might. Walking. Walking. This is the bad thing, and I am here to put a stop to it.

With each lap around the deadly boat, I grow braver and fiercer. Then, concentrating all my energy, all my power in my leg, my foot, I kick the oar Gorman has let go of from its oarlock and watch it fly up in the air and then hit the water with a clunk. Old wood, soggy wood, it hovers in Gorman's sight for a moment, just out of his reach, and then it drifts down and away.

I watch the ferry. So slow. So slow. Was it slowing down?

"Gorman! You hear me? Get back! Go home!"

I notice a stopper on the floor of the boat near the stern. It seems that I am no longer able to make decisions, to choose, to ponder. Suddenly I am carried along, as though by my own strong current. Everything is clear and sharp. It is as though I have been put on this boat for one reason alone, and my whole being is concentrated on what I have to do next.

I think of my hands, of my wrists, of the little

swirling glyphs on my palms. Now the inner patterns of my hands come to life as though carrying out their instructions, knowing what to do. I brace my cold wet feet against the floor of the boat, and with a steady strength, I grasp the old rusted stopper with both my hands and pull.

Despite the cold, I break out in a sweat from sheer concentration. While pulling and twisting, I look up to see if the ferry is still there, but now all I can see are its stern lights slipping away from us. In the distance I think I hear a police siren.

Gorman has stopped rowing, stopped trying to retrieve the lost oar. He has turned his attention to my mother, and like a monkey mother handling her baby roughly, he lifts her by her forearm to sit on his thigh. Her sobs have turned to whimpers and hiccoughs. She is limp and pale against his darkness. Seeing her so, I cannot bear it and without knowing how, I give the plug a final twist. It crumples in my grasp, and suddenly a geyser of cold bay water gushes straight up, hitting me in the face and knocking me backward.

It is then that I realize Gorman can see me, or

perhaps it is only then that I appear to him. His stunned expression quickly turns to rage, and tossing my mother behind him, he comes at me with open hands like claws, heavy, strong, but he is not sure whether to kill me or to press his hands over the bursting rocket of water that is quickly filling the boat.

Behind him I see my mother stand up on the seat, fists pressed to her eyes, her mouth wailing wide, and as Gorman lurches toward me, the boat pitches; and for the rest of my life I will never tip a glass off a table and onto the floor without seeing the image of my mother, the young child, tip and spill into the bay.

Someone screams. It must be me. I leap past Gorman, half through him, half over him, and dive in after my mother. I am thinking that I have not saved her from any bad thing after all, only led her into a different bad thing. I do not know how to be in water. I am not completely solid. So nothing feels like it would feel if I were whole. I don't float. I don't sink. I seem to be lying on top of the water, face pressed to its surface, seeing my mother beneath me, pulled down by her coat, her heavy shoes, and my arms are reaching for her, swirling, swirling, but not reaching her. I see her little face screwed up, bubbles rising, growing farther and farther away from me. I hear Gorman crying, sputtering, and on the edge of my vision, I can see the boat low in the water, sinking lower and lower.

Not knowing how to be in water, but knowing how to be in love, I force myself to follow the bubbles down into the darkness, their very surfaces bursting in my face and filling my senses with her breath. And then a peace comes over me, a warmth that I have never felt before. It is then that I know I have passed over completely. And that my mother is waiting for me. I can save her.

Before I know what has happened my fingers are entwined in hers, like fleshy seaweed pods, cool and soft, and with unexpected ease I pull her up to me and feel her arms slip around my neck.

I come up quickly and we burst like skyrockets through the surface of the water; and I don't know how, but now I am walking across the bay, my feet slapping on the surface of the water, my mother tight in my arms. I am walking toward the shore, and toward the blinking red and yellow lights that have appeared there.

THIRTEEN

I can see my grandmother scrambling down the bank and out into the water, crying out, "Jessie! Jessie!" and somehow my grandfather is there also, swimming beside me toward the shore, and he's shouting too, almost screaming, "I've got her! I've got her!" and when I look down I see the child in the loop of his arm. I see his feet touch bottom, gain ground, and then he and my grandmother meet in a hard collision of panic and love. They both seem to crack wide open into relieved sobs when the child between them wails.

"Oh, darlin', darlin'," my grandmother croons.

"Watch it now," a man shouts. He and another

man are running down the bank with an inflated rescue raft. In what seems like one movement they jump in, start a small motor, and then pass through me with a *whoosh* that takes them out toward Gorman.

All is darkness. There is only the noise of the motor. I turn and look out over the oily dark water. The metal boat is gone. Gorman is gone.

I should have been free then. Somehow I should have turned, rolled, and awakened in my bed back at the cabin, or suddenly opened my eyes and found myself beside the lifeguard chair on the shore with everyone else. It should have been that easy, like passing from one day into the next, my most direct route home. But instead I found myself growing heavier as though I were being weighed down by time, being cemented permanently in the night of my mother's ordeal. There seemed to be no road back to camp for me, no trip across the bay to Jedidiah. The night did not open up and draw me in to deposit me on the lake. Nothing happened.

I looked down at my legs, ankle deep in water, a solitary night fish swimming beneath me in a pale luminescence. I was growing heavy, sinking bit by bit with the weight of time.

I stared out at the rescue lights bouncing along the dark crust of the water. I could see they were in the wrong place. Many yards from where they were, and very deep, I could see Gorman's boat drifting down, down. I dreaded what I was going to have to do, but maybe it was the only way home. Maybe there's only so much you can do to the moments of someone's life. So much good, or so much damage.

Looking back one more time, I watched my grandparents scrambling up the bank with my mother held tight in their arms. I was hoping my mother would look up at me, see me, and wave, but she didn't. I whispered good-bye, and turning, waded out away from them. By the time I stood directly above the sunken boat I was up to my thighs in water. I was growing heavy with the life and time that I was in. I couldn't tell if I was running out of time or drowning in it, but when I looked straight down between my feet, I could see the metal boat far below, settling on the mud at the bottom, and I could see Gorman lying across the floor of the boat, moving slightly. His arm seemed to beckon me. Was he dead? Was he waiting for me?

The rescue boat was too far away. "Here!" I called, but my voice was weak, nothing more than the dim leap and splash of a night fish. "Here!" I tried again, but it was no use. I would have to go alone. So, as though I were whole and as though I were truly there, and maybe I was, I held my breath, jumped and dove down into the dark bay, down and down, closer and closer to Gorman. The currents tossed him about and I tried not to look at his terrible face, his mouth open, his eyes nearly bursting, but surely dead. How long had it been? Two minutes? Five? Ten?

I hesitated, holding my breath. And then I saw it—the starfish on the floor of the boat. It had seemed so familiar before, and now I thought I recognized it. I drew closer. It seemed so familiar. Surely it was mine. Surely it was the very starfish I had found at the lake. The one that had no reason for being there. Five-pointed, rough to the touch with a small V-shaped nick gouged in one of its stout triangular legs.

It was! And I was certain that the starfish was back at the camp. So if I were to hold it, if I could just hold it tight in both my hands, surely I would be back at camp too. I reached for it then, letting my breath escape from my aching lungs in excitement, ready to lurch for the surface, but Gorman's huge hands suddenly reached out to me, grabbed me by my shirt, my hair. I fought him off, hitting him hard, kicking him, beating him off, bubbles and churning water all about us, until I managed to twist myself around, and all he held was one ankle. I lurched along the bottom of the boat, grasped the starfish in my hand, and then with all my strength, I turned toward the surface and tried to swim straight up.

I could see the searchlights crisscrossing in arcs above me. I was strong. My strength did not depend upon which time I was in. My strength was my own, not anchored in any moment, not subject to conditions, or circumstance. I was strong. Tremendously strong, and with that thought alone, I dragged myself to the surface, with Gorman hanging on to me like an anchor full of sludge.

I lifted out of the water like a porpoise, soundless, weightless, and Gorman burst upward after me with such a roar that the men on the rescue boat shouted in fear.

But I didn't stay. My sudden strength didn't lessen. Something was happening to me, and as I had broken through the surface of the water, I continued to burst, as though bursting and bursting, over and over with strength and power and some hidden reservoir of an intensity I have never again felt. I found myself racing across the bay. Racing like the wind with my feet kicking up a spray behind me. Ahead I could make out the running lights of a small sloop, sails wide and lazy, heading across the nighttime bay. I didn't stop. I could make out two people sitting side by side along the cockpit and I saw them stand and stare at me. I laughed wildly and thought how they would later tell their friends they had seen a ghost on the bay, a young girl running along the surface of the water. I laughed and laughed and never stopped. Somehow I knew I was running home.

The lights of the sloop faded behind me and a contentment settled on me, but I continued to run with only the wind in my ears. The familiar shore of the bay faded into night and into years, the familiar stars came out and spun above me, the night breeze caressed my face and welcomed me home. Then up ahead, an amazing thing happened. Fireworks began to light the sky and the water. All colors exploding, crashing, cascading down into the water with stars and moon as backdrop. It was beautiful. It was the last night of camp.

Silhouetted in darkness in a cascade of showering pinks and oranges and blues, I saw the sharp outline of a canoe. A dark canoe that seemed to be waiting, turning expectantly, turning, waiting. I slowed. I walked deliberately and slowly, my breath heavy and deep, clutching the starfish in my hand. As I drew closer, I could see a boy in the canoe. A boy perched on the seat, still, tense, searching the distant shore.

"Jedidiah," I whispered and I stood still. Stood on water. Still. Still. And as he turned to me, and as his teeth flashed white against his face and the night sky, I suddenly felt myself dropped like a cannonball into the water. Laughing! Laughing!

Jed's paddle lifted like a wing, and he came after me.

"Is it over?" he whispered as he pulled me aboard. "Have you had enough? Is it over?"

"It's over," I answered. "It's over."

FOURTEEN

There are no simple endings. Maybe there are no *endings*, period. There are just intricate, elaborate tales that never really finish, that are played out over and over again until they are smooth as beach glass. So the story of my mother and me never really ended either.

The next day when the parents came up to pick up their kids, I sat by myself on the fence and watched up the road. Jedidiah's parents had already come for him and he was gone. We had made a pact, Jed and myself, that once we were back home we'd go on as before and never again speak of what had happened up at camp. He promised me he would die with what had happened still locked in his heart, and I promised him it was over. We shook on it. And even laughed. Mrs. Seger was reluctant to leave me there, but I promised her my grandparents would be along any minute and that I would see her and Jed back at school in a week. I helped Jed load his trunk into the car and watched him drive away, his face in the back window of his parents' car, but invisible to me because of the sunlight.

From my perch on the fence I watched the cars coming in and rolling back out. I kept a keen eye out for the truck, and sure enough, like I knew it would, I saw it laboring up the road, kicking up dust and bouncing along. I slid off the fence and waved, searching the dusty windshield for their faces, almost choking with love for them now. I wanted to go home so badly. I wanted to see them old. Wanted to see their wrinkles and their thinning hair. Their hands, their old shoes. I squinted down the road, hopping with anxiety and joy, trying to make out the shapes of their heads in the windshield, and then I saw it. There was a head between them—PopPop driving, Grandma in the passenger seat, and a third person sitting on the wide seat between them. I froze.

They came up alongside where I was, and one of the counselors was signaling them to move along into the lot, so PopPop, slowing down but not stopping, called out his open window for me to meet them there. But I barely heard him, didn't even look at him. I was looking at my mother, and she was looking out at me. Her head was tilted as though she were ducking down to see me better. She raised her hand and fluttered her fingers. Smiled, nodded. The smile and nod she had never given me that night down at the ferry dock when she was finally safe.

I followed behind, my heart racing, my mind leaping in a hundred directions at once. They parked under a wide shade tree, and the doors opened. PopPop was the first out, his arms open to me, and I was drawn into his arms like a moth to a lightbulb on a hot night. PopPop. Grandma was there too, her hands patting my head and my shoulders. I turned to her and realized we were now the same size, for sure. It had been coming for some time, and it was finally here. Over her shoulder I saw my mother stepping down from the cab of the truck. I was struck by how different she looked. She was dressed in a simple yellow dress the color of butter, and her hair, usually severe and twisted in scarves or hidden under wilted hats, was loose and soft, its edge touching along her jawbone.

She stood facing me squarely, searching my face. "Hello, Zoe," she said.

"I'm surprised to see you," I said.

She stepped forward and raised her arms toward me, and I stepped into them, stiff and awkward. We were like two bundles of sticks, not fitting with each other anywhere. But she touched the back of my head with her hand, and my breath stuck in my throat.

"I guess in some way I'm surprised, too," she said.

"Your mother's coming home with us," PopPop said.

"For a visit?" I asked looking from Grandma to PopPop for the answer. Grandma's eyes seemed painfully hopeful.

"No," my mother began. "I'm not sure what it

is, but it's not just a visit. I thought I'd like to try something."

"What?"

She smiled. "Do you remember what you used to tell me to be when you were little?"

I didn't. I couldn't remember ever speaking to her at all when I was little.

"You used to tell me to be your true mother."

I felt my cheeks grow hot. "I used to say that?"

Grandma and PopPop laughed. "You used to say that all the time."

She was smiling at me. Then whispering across the lost time and broken places of both our lives, she said, "But you have to be patient with me, okay? This can be a kind of a beginning for us, if I can do it."

The sun was shining through the leaves above us, giving everything an unreal feeling, a flickering feeling like an old movie in fast-forward, racing forward to what? I wondered.

So, you see? There are no endings, just as there are no simple beginnings, because always we can go back to yet another before, another yesterday, that stands significantly before the last yesterday we know. We can always find those distant moments to point to, to say this here is where it began. And this here is where it's all going. As though time is a vast place that stretches beneath us like a warm sandy bottom of a clear bay.

But all we really have is now, and the best we can do—before that now slips forgotten into our yesterdays—is to press it in the passages of our minds, like a goldenrod pressed between blotters and set beneath the leg of a heavy bed. That way, we can open it someday and remember.

I have saved such a moment. It is early October of that same year, and it is dusk. I am sitting on the back steps at Grandma's, the exact place where a pumpkin once sat, and I am transfixed by the rosy glow of the sky high above me. Through the sparse, newly bare branches of autumn I see a sharp star. I hear the screen door open behind me and I turn to see my mother looking down at me.

"You cold, sweetie?"

"A little. But I'll only be a minute. Look." I point at the star, and together we look up.

Then she says, *"Wish I may, wish I might."*

"Have the wish I wish tonight," I finish for her.

She holds the door open with her hip and hugs her arms around herself. She is not such a young woman anymore, but I think she is still beautiful. And if I squint a little, I can see the child she once was. Then to my amazement my mother says, "I wish that you and I could always be like this, right here, right now, just like this forever."

I don't even breathe. I just stay like that until after a while she says, "It's cold, Zoe. Come on in."

In that next instant, I stand and follow her up the steps into the warmth and brightness of my grandmother's kitchen. I do it for her, but I know that somewhere in time, we are still on the back steps, the two of us, together forever, looking up into the sky, and that image of us is racing up into the stars, even now.

PAM CONRAD has written a number of award-winning novels, including STONEWORDS, winner of the 1991 Edgar Allan Poe Award for Best Juvenile Mystery, and PRAIRIE SONGS, a 1985 SCBW Golden Kite Award Honor Book. She is also the author of several picture books, including DOLL FACE HAS A PARTY!, illustrated by Brian Selznick; ANIMAL LINGO, illustrated by Barbara Falk; and THE TUB PEOPLE, THE TUB GRANDFATHER, THE LOST SAILOR, and most recently, CALL ME AHNIGHITO, all illustrated by Richard Egielski.